The Grown-Up

Jordan Harrison

A Samuel French Acting Edition

SAMUEL
FRENCH

FOUNDED 1830

SAMUELFRENCH.COM
SAMUELFRENCH-LONDON.CO.UK

FOR PRODUCTION ENQUIRIES

UNITED STATES AND CANADA
Info@SamuelFrench.com
1-866-598-8449

UNITED KINGDOM AND EUROPE
Plays@SamuelFrench-London.co.uk
020-7255-4302

Each title is subject to availability from Samuel French, depending upon
country of performance. Please be aware that *THE GROWN-UP* may
not be licensed by Samuel French in your territory. Professional and
amateur producers should contact the nearest Samuel French office or
licensing partner to verify availability.

MUSIC USE NOTE

Licensees are solely responsible for obtaining formal written permission from copyright owners to use copyrighted music in the performance of this play and are strongly cautioned to do so. If no such permission is obtained by the licensee, then the licensee must use only original music that the licensee owns and controls. Licensees are solely responsible and liable for all music clearances and shall indemnify the copyright owners of the play(s) and their licensing agent, Samuel French, against any costs, expenses, losses and liabilities arising from the use of music by licensees. Please contact the appropriate music licensing authority in your territory for the rights to any incidental music.

IMPORTANT BILLING AND CREDIT REQUIREMENTS

If you have obtained performance rights to this title, please refer to your licensing agreement for important billing and credit requirements.

THE GROWN-UP was first produced by the Actors Theatre of Louisville (Les Waters, Artistic Director) in Kentucky as part of the 2014 Humana Festival. The performance was directed by Ken Rus Schmoll, with sets by David Zimmerman, costumes by Janice Pytel, lights by Paul Toben, and sound and original music by Lindsay Jones. The Production Stage Manager was Katie Shade. The cast was as follows:

ACTOR A	Matthew Stadelmann
ACTOR B	Brooke Bloom
ACTOR C	Paul Niebanck
ACTOR D	Tiffany Villarin
ACTOR E	Chris Murray
ACTOR F	David Ryan Smith

CHARACTERS

ACTOR A – Kai *(rhymes with eye)*

ACTOR B – Anna Bell / Lane Heatherette

ACTOR C – Grandfather / First Mate / Barry / Minister

ACTOR D – Grandma / Rosie / Wedding Guest / Paula

ACTOR E – Mr. See / Wedding Planner / Award Ceremony Emcee

ACTOR F – Josef the Fisherman / Steven / Cater Waiter / Miss McGinn

AUTHOR'S NOTES

There is a strange kind of blindness to this play, not unlike a radio play. Hopefully this can be liberating: we can go anywhere – a tall ship in a storm, a crowded ballroom – because we don't have to see these places realized. We can be any age. I suspect that there is very little on stage.

All of the actors do narrating duty. Narrated lines are *set in italics* for the sake of readability, but they are very much within the action and momentum of the scene. They are not a step outside; they are not direct-address.

Because the costume changes are minimal and the characters plentiful, the actors are always actors in a sense – which is maybe why it seemed right to identify them as Actor A, Actor B, etc.

I.

A. It doesn't *look* very valuable,

B. *you say.*

A. Looks like glass.

C. Crystal,

B. *your grandfather says, running his fingers over the doorknob.*

C. You can tell by the way the light is trapped. How it's split into rainbows, here?

A. Oh yeah,

B. *you lie. You don't want him to know you can't see. There's something wrong with people who can't see magic.*

C. It's older than this house. It's older than me. It's even older than your grandma.

D. Older than Grandma? Impossible!,

B. *Grandma says. And back to her knitting.*

C. I reckon it's older than this whole country.

A. How do you know?

B. *You squint but it still looks like glass.*

C. The man who built this house—When I was your age he was my age, if you follow. Real geezer, with one bad eye the color of an iceberg.

B. *Grandfather's eyes pass over the old ship's wheel mounted on the wall.*

C. He was just an ordinary fisherman, but long before, he'd been a cabin boy on a tallship. That's how he came across it.

A. The ship was carrying doorknobs?

C. Treasure, from the Silk Road. Spices, incense. *Jewels,*

B. *he adds, strategically. Spices are abstract to a ten-year-old, but jewels—*

C. *(To* **A.***)* They figured to make a fortune, but half of them died on the way here, from scarlet scurvy.

D. Fever.

C. What?

D. Scarlet fever.

C. You weren't there.

A. Does scarlet scurvy make you scarlet?

C. Not anymore, thank god. They put an end to it long before you were born.

B. *And you're glad to hear it, though the idea of a disease disappearing altogether is somehow troubling—like your favorite TV show ending, or a whole species ending, or* you *ending.*

C. Anyhow—

B. *Grandfather lights his pipe–*

C. The old sailor said the doorknob was part of his ship, once. You know all those ships had a lady on the prow, a chesty lady.

D. A mermaid—

C. A chesty mermaid.

D. George, don't say "chesty."

C. What should I say? Popular?

B. *Grandma drops a stitch.*

D. Look what you made me do.

C. Now this ship wasn't just any ship...

A. It was a pirate ship.

C. How do you know?

A. Why else would it have a story about it.

B. *Grandfather doesn't like how certain you are.*

C. Maybe it wasn't a pirate ship after all.

A. No, it was!

C. Maybe it was a tugboat.

A. *(Pleading.)* It *was* a pirate ship, it was!

C. *(Relenting.)* So it was. But before they could reach Portsmouth—when they were out in the deepest part of the ocean, the ship was eaten whole by a great wave.

D. I thought you said scarlet fever.

C. First fever, then the wave.

D. Very unlucky pirates,

B. *Grandma says.*

C. The unluckiest.

B. *Even at age ten, you sense there's something fun for them in these little battles.*

C. Can't you just imagine all those silks and doubloons sinking to the ocean floor? What a goddamn waste. And the hell of it was—

D. George—

C. The heck of it was, the only part of that whole great ship that survived, the only thing that washed ashore was the big round crystal in the eye of the chesty mermaid on the prow. And do you know where that eye ended up?

B. *You look over at the doorknob.*

A. No way!

B. *And he's got you now. There's a little itch down the back of your neck like the fingernail of a ghost.*

A. What's so special about a doorknob?

B. *you say, covering.*

C. *(With mystic intrigue.)* It's a doorknob to anywhere.

A. A doorknob to anywhere? What's that supposed to mean?

C. It means if ever you're feeling a little bored with your smart-ass ten-year-old self; if ever you're getting tired of playing gin rummy with your sister; if ever you're feeling like summer is going altogether too slow, then you just go over and grip that doorknob very hard with both hands—

D. George, he'll think you're serious.

C. Just pull 'til it pops clean off. Then you stick that knob on any door you want, and the second the door opens you'll be someplace else.

A. Where?

C. That's the catch.

A. There's *always* a catch,

B. *you say, flopping back onto the couch in a way that makes Grandfather narrow his eyes, wondering if you aren't a future homosexual.*

C. The catch, since you asked, is that you can't choose where the doorknob will take you. The doorknob doesn't care about time and space, life or death. Death doesn't trouble it. You could end up a thousand miles away, or a hundred years ago. You could end up somewhere that will make you beg for your little sister and gin rummy.

D. Stop scaring the boy.

A. I'm not scared.

B. *Yes you are.*

C. You're very young. You could stand to be a little scared.

B. *Some of the light and love seems to leave his eyes, but you're not sure what's replaced it.*

A. If it's a magic doorknob, then how come I've seen Grandma open that closet a million times and there's nothing in it but placemats and napkins and stuff?

C. That's on account of it's the Safety Door.

A. The Safety Door?

C. Like neutral for a car. It's the one door where you can put the doorknob when you want it to be just a doorknob. The one door where its powers don't work.

D. How convenient,

B. *Grandmother says. She looks up from her knitting, hearing footsteps.*

> (**ACTOR D** *looks at* **ACTOR B** *for the first time.*
> **ACTOR B** *is now* **ANNA BELL**.)

D. Well look who's here, Kai. If it isn't your poor little sister, looking for a friend.

B. Gin rummy?

A. Not now.

E. *Anna Bell always wins at gin rummy. Always.*

B. Why not now?

A. I'm talking to Grandpa.

B. What about?

A. You're not old enough.

B. *(A second opinion.)* Grandpa?

C. I'm afraid he's right.

E. *(To A.) You and Grandfather share a look. You are never so close as when you're leaving Anna Bell out.*

B. Whatever it is, I bet it's stupid.

D. Yes, dear. It is stupid.

B. Why does Kai keep looking at that door?

D. Never mind that.

Sit down and I'll teach you the garter stitch.

II.

(The **FISHERMAN** *stands under a lamppost. It is raining lightly.* **ACTOR A** *stands outside of the light as he narrates:)*

A. *An old Fisherman squints into the darkness.*

F. Hello?

A. *There's someone out there, just beyond his vision. He could see who if it weren't for his one bad eye the color of an iceberg.*

(The **FISHERMAN** *tunes a little pocket radio that plays a sea shanty:)*

RADIO.

ARE YOU MISSIN' THE SEA?
SOMETIMES LIKE YOUR MOTHER

ARE YOU MISSIN' THE SEA?
SOMETIMES NOT AT ALL
ARE YOU MISSIN' THE SEA?
LIKE A LIMB THAT YOU LOST
ARE YOU MISSIN' THE WAY
IT MAKES YOU FEEL SMALL.

> *(He turns the knob on the radio and finds a different station.)*

OH YOU BATTEN THE STAYSAIL AND GAZE AT THE STARS
AND WONDER, ARE WE MEANT TO SEE THAT FAR...

> *(This one seems to stir up bad memories. He turns the knob. Another song:)*

STORM A-COMING TONIGHT,
LET EVERY MAN KNOW.
SWING LEFT, SWING RIGHT
HITCH YOUR HAMMOCK UP TIGHT
SWING HIGH, SWING LOW
SWEET DREAMS OF A GIRL IN A RED TROUSSEAU.

> *(The **FISHERMAN** tries to see who's out there in the darkness. Squinting in the direction of **ACTOR A**:)*

F. Anybody out there?

A. *No answer.*

F. Come say hello if you want.

> *(Beat.)*

(Muttering, giving up.) Be a nice change.

III.

B. Gin!

E. *cries Anna Bell. She's won the last six games.*

A. I don't believe you.

E. *She shows you her cards.*

B. *(Showing him the win.)* One, two, three.

E. *She smiles. Her teeth are black with licorice.*

B. Play again?

A. Let me win this time?

B. No.

A. Then no.

B. *(Whining.)* There's two whole hours to dinner.

A. We could play something else.

B. Like what.

A. How about *Grossest Thing You Can Think Of.* Or *Where Did My Eyelids Go.*

B. You always win those games.

A. Or *Find My Booger.* I'll give you a hint—it's under your pillow.

B. Mom, Kai won't play normal!

A. *(To B.)* Shut up!

E. *It might be the most penetrating thing she's ever said: Kai won't play normal.*

B. Mom! Kai told me to shut up!

A. Shut up!

E. *You peek into the doorknob room, which is also your grandparents' sitting room. Empty now.*

D. *Grandma is cooking supper.*

C. *Grandfather is puttering around the garage.*

B. I'm bored.

E. *You get an idea.*

A. How 'bout we play hide-and-seek? You can hide first.

B. That's how you always get rid of me when you want to get rid of me.

A. I promise, Anna Bell,

E. *you lie.*

A. Anna Bell, my favorite only sister, I promise I'll come find you.

B. Okay, count to a hundred.

A. Fifty.

B. That's too short!

A. One,

E. *you say, and she's off and running. Off to the toy chest in the attic, her favorite hiding place. Never mind you've found her there before.*

B. *(Heartbreakingly, all she really wants is to be found.)*

E. *And there's nothing worse than giving her what she wants.*

A. Two, three, four...

E. *You make your voice a little louder to cover the fact that you're slipping into the next room. Reverse Doppler.*

A. Five! Six!

C. *Your hand on the crystal doorknob now, the doorknob to anywhere.*

E. *Does it give off a faint glow, or is it just your imagination?*

D. *You pull it off the safety door with a satisfying pop.*

A. Seven! Eight!

C. *Pick a door, any door...*

D. *Front door?*

C. *Nah*

A. No

E. *Maybe.*

D. *The front door has little glass windows. You can see the sunny day beyond, the climbing tree, Anna Bell's purple plastic ponies mouldering on the lawn.*

C. *Yes, <u>this</u> door. Not a crooked little gnomish door, but an everyday door: The perfect test for a magic doorknob.*

A. Nine! Ten!

E. *You put the knob on the door—*

D. *It slides over the real one with magic ease—*

C. *The knob turns in your hand, and the door opens*

B. Kai? You were up to ten and you stopped.
Kai?

C. *And you step on through.*

(Continuous into...)

IV.

E. *(Cordial.)* Kai!

F. *You enter the bright office.*

E. Welcome.

F. *Big desk with a man behind it. Sun in your eyes not his.*

E. Sorry to make you wait.

A. Oh no, it wasn't—It was actually good to have a little breather after the traffic, which was—

E. Yeah, welcome to L.A. How long were you waiting?

A. It was my fault, I got here early, so.

E. Yeah you shouldn't do that in this town.

A. I shouldn't?

E. Looks low on the totem pole.

A. Trying too hard.

E. Something like that. Another thing you shouldn't do is pace outside the TV executive's window for twenty minutes practicing your pitch to thin air.

A. You saw that?

F. *Shit.*

E. I was trying not to.

C. *Shit.*

E. Relax, Kai. Can I call you Kai, Kai?

A. Sure.

E. Just relax. Bonnie warned me I was getting an 18-carat New York City neurotic.

A. 24-carat.

E. Hah, whatever. Bonnie sure can pick 'em.

A. Bonnie's great.

E. She's got a real eye for writers. Or is it an ear.

A. Both maybe.

E. She said you were like the new Woody Allen but more, you know…

A. Waspy?

E. No. Woody Allen but with more…

A. *(Off his gesture.) Cojones.*

E. What? What's that?

A. Balls in Spanish.

E. That's it—Woody Allen with balls.

F. *Silence.*

A. Yeah, Bonnie's great.

E. So you wanna go ahead and tell me this thing of yours? Bonnie says you're cookin' up something special.

A. Actually, do you guys have any coffee?

E. *(Preposterous.)* "Do we have coffee." *(Into intercom, but not miming this:)* Rosie, our writer friend wants to know if we have any coffee. *(Back to* A:*)* We have a freezer full of Acid Reflux Roast from Intelligentsia. Know that place?

A. No.

E. You should never admit to not-knowing in this town.

A. Oh, sorry.

E. And never apologize. Kidding!

A. Ha

D. Milk and sugar?

A. Oh, no thanks

E. Thanks, Rosie

A. Thanks.

E. So now you're all parked, you're all coked up on that –

A. Getting there –

E. And you've done a little dance outside my window. Any more stalling you wanna do?

A. Well I just—ha, that's good—I would really just love to hear what you guys do here first. I have a few different ideas so I don't wanna just throw spaghetti against the wall, you know? I wanna hear what you guys are into.

E. First of all, there's no "into," okay? That's what you literary types have to remember. This isn't personal. We're not "into," we're "about."

A. What are you about?

E. Cops, doctors, and lawyers. That's the brand, that's what works for us. You can slice up the series in syndication, shuffle it every which way and Judy Housewife doesn't care if she's watching season three, nine or seventeen, so long as there's a guy in a trench coat looking at some bones. His haircut might change but that's about it. We call it "counter-context programming." Say it for me.

A. I'd rather not.

E. *("Really?")* You're not gonna say it for me.

A. Counter-context programming.

E. See? That wasn't so bad.

A. Great. So, should I just? —

E. No time like the present.

A. Ha. *(Three descending notes:)* Duh-dah-dum.

E. Yeah, I know that, that's *Psycho.*

A. Actually I think *Psycho* is *Ree-ree-ree-ree.* I was doing more like classic Lon Chaney horror I guess, with a soupçon of *Jaws.*

E. This guy's a real movie buff.

A. Well, yeah.

E. *(Lightly condescending.)* No, it's great.

A. So I've been rolling this idea around in my head a lot

E. Good, good...

A. And I mean it's kind of a guilty pleasure but highbrow. Kind of a *Pirates of the Caribbean* meets *Quantum Leap,* but not at all '80s. Very current, good hair... Bonnie told me period is out, so.

E. Period's the worst. Isn't it, Rosie.

D. Hate.

A. Is she gonna keep listening in?

E. That a problem?

A. I guess not.

E. So: *Quantum Leap* plus pirates

A. Well the hero is this guy who's like the opposite of a pirate. Like the guy from *Sideways,* whatshisname

E. Oh I love him

A. But with more sex appeal

E. *(Obviously.)* Yeah.

A. But still, you know, normal

E. Rick something

A. *("No.")* Something like that

E. What's the guy's name Rosie

D. Paul Giamatti

E. *Giamatti.* Tip of my tongue.

A. And he plays this guy who gets time-jumped back

E. *There's* Quantum Leap

A. He has to right a wrong from his family's past or something

E. *(Liking this more.)* Okay, okay. Revenge is stupid right now.

A. Revenge is "stupid"?

E. Oh sorry, that means "hot." I see how that could be confusing.

A. So our guy, he ends up back on a 19th century pirate ship –

E. Why a pirate ship?

A. *(He realizes he doesn't know.)* I guess I just like pirates.

E. Stop. *(The best idea ever:)* What if they were *modern* pirates, like Somali pirates.

A. I don't think so

E. But you said not period

A. Just trust me on this. So our hero finds himself in this life that's not his own—He has to man the crow's nest, he has to survive a shipwreck, maybe he gets himself a parrot

E. This is TV we're talking about?

A. Yeah, why

E. Feels Feature to me. Does it feel Feature to you Rose?

D. Feels feature.

E. See?

A. Feels feature why?

E. Time stuff is easier to pull off on the big screen. Big canvas, bright colors. Like *Jacuzzi Time Flux*, you see that?

A. *(Politic.)* I saw the ads.

E. That thing set records. *(Significantly.)* On the big screen.

A. I was kind of seeing one-hour drama. Well, drame*dy*.

E. That's a word we like. That's a good word here.

A. As I was saying the pirate is kind of a sad-sack, like an office worker, a janitor

E. *(Helpfully.)* A writer

A. Yeah—*Hey*

E. Kidding, go on.

A. Say, what's that on your desk?

E. What, the paperweight?

A. Is it glass?

E. Crystal, I think. My last assistant gave it to me.

A. I saw something like that once. I don't know where.

E. Nice girl, totally burned out on me. That's how it goes with these girls. They come in all ready to grab the world by the—what was that word?

A. *Cojones*

E. Ready to kick the world in the *cojones*, but then they just *(He makes a gesture for disappearing in a puff of smoke.)* You still listening in, Rose?

D. Sure am, Mr. See.

E. Don't burn out on me, 'kay Rosie girl?

D. Not the plan, Mr. See.

E. Isn't she great?

A. Mr. See, how old do I look to you?

E. Early-late twenties I'd say, but your skin's good for a writer. Bonnie said you could pass for late-early twenties, and she wasn't wrong.

A. *(Almost to himself.)* I was talking to my grandfather—it was yesterday. It was today. I was ten.

E. You okay, Kai? You look confused.

A. What did he tell me. "If you're ever bored…"

E. Could be the coffee—Not everyone can handle the Reflux Roast. Right Rosie?

> **(ROSIE** *is strangely paralyzed—like an actor who's forgotten her lines.)*

Rosie, you make the coffee too strong again?

> *(Still no answer.)*

A. *(With new resolve.)* I know what this is.

E. Again with the paperweight.

A. It's not a paperweight.

E. Are you *trying* to throw this meeting? Or do they like bullshit back in New York?

A. I went through a door. How did I forget?

E. Don't touch that!

A. That must be part of it—the forgetting

E. This isn't coffee. Lemme guess: you're the new kid in town, you snort a few uppers, don't know how to handle it—

A. *(Piecing it together, in his own world.)* I'm a boy, I'm ten. I'm playing gin rummy with my sister.

E. Rosie, get security. Rosie?

A. I'll go back. Maybe if I turn it the opposite way—

E. Put the doorknob DOWN.

A. I thought you said it was a paperweight.

F. *Silence.*

E. Kai, / listen—

A. *(Overlapping.)* Stay away from me.

C. *You move toward the door.*

E. Whatever's on the other side of that door, it's not your sister playing gin rummy. It's not your grandfather and his pipe. It's farther down the path—infinitely worse.

A. How can it be worse than here,

F. *you say, turning your back*

C. *And he's up from his desk, his hands reaching for you*

F. *But you're faster, you're younger*

C. *You're twisting the knob and you're safe*

F. *You're safe*

C. *You're gone.*

E. Rosie!

V.

*(The **OLD FISHERMAN** stands under the lamppost listening to the radio. Another sea song:)*

RADIO.
STILL HAVEN'T GOT YOUR LAND LEGS
STILL GOT YOUR HANDS ON DECK
SALT IN YOUR HAIR, SALT IN YOUR SHORTS
AND YOU'RE A DOGGONE WRECK.
OHHHHH, STILL HAVEN'T GOT—

*(The **FISHERMAN** changes the station—a little too close to home. Static, nothing but static. Finally he picks something up. The voice of an eight-year-old girl:)*

B. Kai? You promised you'd find me.
Kai? This isn't funny.

*(The radio starts to weep. The **FISHERMAN** turns it off.)*

F. Poor kid.

(He climbs the lamppost like the mast of a ship. As he gets higher, we hear the sound of the ocean. A voice from out of the darkness:)

C. Boy!

(The **FISHERMAN** *closes his eyes and light slowly rises on* **ACTOR C** *as the* **FIRST MATE***.)*

A. *With your eyes shut, the past rushes in—*

C. I said Cabin Boy!

F. *(Eyes shut.)* Up here!

A. *The First Mate takes shape—first his body, then his handlebar mustache, and finally his black-toothed pirate's mouth—like the Cheshire Cat in reverse.*

(The light on **ACTOR C** *completes.)*

C. What do you see up there?

(The **FISHERMAN** *opens his eyes on the horizon.)*

F. Nothing, Sir!

A. *The First Mate narrows his eyes.*

C. If you're gonna man the crow's nest, you have to learn to see better. Nothing is ever nothing.

F. What do you mean?

C. The clouds. Cirrus or altostratus?

F. Sky's clear, Sir!

C. Moon. Gibbous or crescent?

F. No moon!

C. *New* moon. Sign of land?

F. Middle of the ocean, Sir.

C. Waves?

F. Still as a bathtub.

C. That's it, I'm coming up.

A. *He scales the mizzen like a monkey up a tree.*

C. Well I'll be damned.

F. What?

C. Looks a whole lot like nothing.
    Except—

F. Where

C. See that red ribbon where sea meets sky?

F. What is it?

C. Could be nothing. Could be a mean squall headed our way.

F. Is it ever a friendly squall?

C. *(Unsmiling.)* You're a funny kid. You got a mom or a dad?

F. Dead, Sir.

C. Well you've got me now. I think I'll call you Josef. It sounds better than Cabin Boy.

F. Josef.

C. Never had a son,

A. *The First Mate says. His eyes are wet, but they stay fixed on the sky.*

F. Sir? Is this really happening?

A. *The image of the First Mate starts to swim a little. You shut your eyes tight, holding onto the memory.*

C. What do you mean, really happening?

F. Because I miss you—but you're right here.

C. 'Course I'm here,

A. *he says, eyeing the red ribbon on the horizon.*

F. It's getting wider. Is that good?

C. It's not good.

A. *You watch it grow 'til it eats half the sky.*

C. Feel that wind?

F. Yeah.

C. That wind's bringing rain.

VI.

(When B, C, *and* F *speak for* ROSIE, *they look directly at her.)*

B. *Eff me,*

D. Rosie says to herself as she presses her brand-new espadrille slingbacks on the gas and merges across four lanes of traffic to the carpool lane of the 405.

She's propped up the mannequin torso her sister got her from the SkyMall catalog for the purpose of masquerading as two people in the carpool lane. Cut her commute nearly in half. Thanks, Sis.

Rosie presses harder with her espadrille slingbacks. She speeds. Trying to outrun the stinging awareness that she's let down Mr. See. It is the job of the assistant not merely to brew delicious coffee and deflect unwanted calls and to sparkle like a fine hard gem, but also to maintain whatever reality is called for on any given day, with any given subject.

C. *Dammit,*

D. Rosie says, pulling into the driveway.

F. *Eff me,*

D. she cries as she washes the kale, juliennes the jicama slaw and brings the quinoa to a slow boil all at the same time.

B. *Effing eff!*

D. she shouts as she pulverizes two Adderall with a spoon and sprinkles the Adderall dust on top of the kale, and puts the kale in her mouth.

B. *That*

C. *Effing*

F. *Doorknob.*

D. It's true, the real effover of this job is that the magic totem in question has to be present in each reality, present like DNA. Be it wand, broom, enchanted flute, or in this case, magic doorknob, the object has to reside out in the open. Hidden in plain view. Magic is so arbitrary—it can be very annoying. Still, a more seasoned assistant would have hidden it better, in plainer view. Right under his nose maybe. (In the coffee mug? On the seat of his seat?)

At the very least she might have furnished Mr. See with a diversion as the subject, Kai Shearwater, started to get his bearings, to remember his base reality. That was known to happen from time to time—they covered it in the training manual. Instead she froze up. She hasn't froze up like that since the time Lane Heatherette spilled her 'tini on her on purpose at the Palm Springs New Gen Networkathon.

F. *Dammit Rosie you're better than this.*

D. At least Mr. See knows her heart is in it. How does he know her heart is in it? The other day he was asking her, Rosie, what's it like being on Adderall. And Rosie said she didn't want to sound *conceited*, but one time she was in the finals of the Miss Junior Executive of Arkansas Pageant?

E. *Rosie, you hick!*

D. Mr. See joked.

E. *I knew you had a little southern twang, but Arkansas? You fucking backwater hick!*

D. They were always joking like that. And Rosie went on to explain how she'd been in the Final Five Round, the question round, after doing her utmost-most in evening wear, swimwear, and her stand-up routine with Lazy Sue her ventriloquist dummy who likes rabbi jokes, and how the judges asked her,

F. *Rosie, here in the final round of the Miss Junior Executive of Arkansas Pageant, what would you like to give the world if you become Miss Junior Executive?*

D. and how they meant not just giving to Arkansas but to the non-Arkansas world also, and how she replied first with "I'm glad you asked that question," which is a time-honored time-buying strategy, and then how she calmly answered, "*Me,* Sir. I would give the world all of me, down to the capillary, down to the hot-oiled hair follicle," and the crowd was on its feet, all except for her nemesis Lane Heatherette.

And *that,* long story short, is what it's like to be on Adderrall, when every second is like, I'm gonna give all of me, me, me to you, Mr. See, See, See. I'll give my all to Arkansas, and to non-Arkansas, and to the sad runners-up of the pageant, and even to that poor confused man with the crystal doorknob. The whole world is going to get all of Rosie, and then someday, although she doesn't like to sound conceited, someday the whole world will be hers in return.

E. *You're gonna shine Rosie,*

E & C. *Shine Rosie,*

E, C, B. *Shine girl,*

E, C, B, F. *Shine.*

VII.

B. *On the other side of the door from that bright office, it's the middle of the night.*

E. *You kick off the sticky covers.*

F. You awake?

A. No. You?

F. It's too hot to sleep.

B. *You can just make out the glow of the sad little Milky Way someone stuck on the ceiling, its charge almost gone.*

A. I was thinking about what happens when we die.

F. What did you figure out?

A. It doesn't look good.

(*Beat.*)

F. What made you think of that?

A. I'm going to be *forty*, Steven.

F. In a year.

A. A year is nothing. (*Beat.*)
...Also my grandpa.

F. I thought your grandpa died when you were in college.

A. He did, but—Have you ever known someone who always seemed so alive that it's weird that they're not?—I'm too tired for this conversation.

E. *You look out the window.*

> (**ACTOR C** *comes out of the darkness, looking like* **GRANDFATHER.**)

C. *There's an old man coming out of the 24-hour bodega who looks like he could be your grandfather.*

A. He'd be over a hundred now.

F. How old was he when he died?

> (**ACTOR C** *putters back into the darkness, an anonymous old man again.*)

A. Eighty-seven. He had a good life.

F. Buddhists think death is just another beginning.

A. Buddhists are bullshit.

F. It's kind of sexy when you're a dumb mouth-breathing thug.

A. Steven.

F. What.

A. It's too hot.

F. You smell good.

A. I don't feel like I smell good.

F. Well I don't mean like a *rose garden.* You smell like the cigarette you thought I wouldn't notice you had earlier but it stuck to you.

A. So: dumb, thuggish and guilty. That's really a—that's quite a mandala of desire you have going on. Why not throw in some whips and chains just to lighten things up?

F. No objections here.

B. *There's an invitation in this which you don't accept.*

E. *Still he's moving toward you across the bed, this full grown man is on you, his mouth on your neck, his weight on your cock, your cock growing—You're a grown man too, it turns out.*

B. *The cat runs from the room, terrified. You hadn't noticed it 'til now.*

E. *And you're not sure what to do—Have you done this before? Is this your body?—But Steven knows what to do and his mouth is on you and the world*

  falls

  away

  Ok you're back. The room is even hotter now.

A. What's wrong.

F. Nothing's wrong.

A. If you want me to do something different just say so.

F. I don't want something different.

A. I'm too old.

F. No

A. I'm too old for you.

F. I like too old for me, so lucky you.

A. Did you ever think you'd be with someone who could be a grandfather?

F. You couldn't

A. Sure I could—if I had my kid young, and my kid had a kid.

> *(Beat.)*

I can feel my bones. That can't be good.

F. What kind of a name is Kai?

A. I see what you're doing

F. What am I doing

A. Distracting me. We've been together, what / now

F. Fifteen months

A. And all of a sudden you're asking about my name?

F. We can still small-talk, can't we? Or do we have to just talk about death.

> *(Beat.)*

A. It's Scandinavian. It's the name of the boy in *The Snow Queen.*

F. Hans Christian Andersen.

A. Ja.

F. Remind me how it goes?

A. Um, there's this evil queen

F. *You're* an evil queen

A. *(Facetiously, exaggeratedly gay.)* Werq!

F. Werq!

A. There's an evil queen, and she breaks this mirror, on purpose or not I forget, and the pieces go flying out into the world. But it's a twisted mirror, a fun-house mirror that makes everything look dark and mean. There's a little boy—Kai—and his sister.

F. What's the sister's name?

> *(**ACTOR B** is close by right now. **ACTOR A** looks right through her:)*

A. I don't remember. So the little boy gets a piece of mirror stuck in his eye and everything looks dark and mean. And he becomes like the disciple of the evil queen, like he drives her carriage or something.

F. If it's snow then it's a sleigh.

A. Fine, a sleigh. And he's her footman or whatever, he doesn't even remember his sister. It's like his childhood is stolen. They never say that in the story exactly but it scared the shit out of me as a kid. The protagonist is just suddenly...not the protagonist anymore—It's kind of radical actually.

F. That's such a writer thing to say.

A. Poor you. Boyfriends with a writer.

B. *The cat has returned. She runs her wet nose along your hand.*

F. How does it end?

A. His sister goes looking for him— *(Maybe we notice* **ACTOR B** *hearing this.)* And she like beats the Snow Queen and wins him back in the end.

F. Of course.

A. "Of course"?

F. It's a fairy tale.

A. Hans Christian Andersen is different. It's, like, bleeding mermaids

F. Oh yeah

A. So happy's a departure.

F. *(Absently trying this phrase on.)* "Happy's a departure."

    (Beat.)

A. *(Grave news.)* Picador doesn't want the book.

F. What? They told you?

A. This afternoon.

F. You didn't say anything

    (Beat.)

    What did they tell you?

A. They want more fantasy stories, they don't want memoir. Never mind the writing's gotten better.

F. Nadra didn't fight for you?

A. Not enough, apparently.

F. Oh baby.

A. What if I'm not supposed to do this, Steven.

F. Don't be crazy

A. What if I was really supposed to be in data entry but too many people told me I *had* something but they were just being nice and now it's too late—

F. It's one rejection

A. It's a mountain of rejection.

B. *All of a sudden, you feel something under your pillow*

E. *What is that*

A. What *is* that?

F. What's what.

A. There's like a rock. Under my pillow.

F. It's like a cheesy new age crystal.

A. Turn on the light.

F. Maybe it's your crazy ex, casting a spell on you.

A. Who, Richie?

F. I don't know his name.

A. Yes you do.

F. He never got over you.

A. It's not Richie. *(Beat.)* How the fuck did this get under my pillow.

F. It's really weird.

A. Is it a doorknob? I can feel the screws.

> (**KAI** *closes his eyes tight. Warm light rises on* **C** *and* **D** *playing* **GRANDFATHER** *and* **GRANDMA**, *as before.*)

D. *With your eyes shut, you can see your Grandma knitting and rocking, knitting and rocking.*

C. *You can see your Grandfather, lighting his pipe for dramatic emphasis.*

A. It was yesterday. It was today. It just happened.

F. What just happened, baby?

> (**KAI** *opens his eyes and* **C** *and* **D** *disappear.*)

A. I'm not your baby.

F. Kai, what the fuck?

A. What if you're just like him

F. Him who?

A. That TV executive, Mr. See. What if you're trying to keep me from remembering?

F. I'm getting your Lexapro.

A. How old am I, Steven?

F. Settle down.

A. How old am I!

F. Thirty-nine.

A. I was in my twenties.

F. Weren't we all.

A. I mean—this morning.

F. *(Re: the medicine.)* Did you skip a day again?

A. *(Not re: the medicine.)* I skipped more than a day.

F. You know you can't do that.

A. I was this kid going to LA for meetings…

F. Baby, everybody gets old.

A. Pitching some awful show with pirates

F. You had a bad day, that's all. Here, swallow.

A. *(Preoccupied.)* It was today. It was this morning.

F. Swallow.

A. *(He doesn't.)* He had a crystal, just like this one. Not a crystal—a doorknob.

E. *You eye the door to the closet.*

A. What happens if I go through another?

F. Another what?

A. *(To himself.)* He said "farther down the path"

F. I'm calling your therapist

A. What if it only goes farther, not back

E. *Your hand on the doorknob.*

F. *(Trying to talk reason.)* Kai. This is me. That's you. That's our cat. This is our life.

A. Then why does everything feel wrong?

(Beat.)

A. Goodbye, Steven.

E. *The doorknob turns*

F. What do you mean, goodbye? That's the closet.

A. Wish me luck.

(Light shifts. Continuous into:)

VIII.

(ACTOR F is suddenly a young CATER WAITER with a tray of hors d'oeuvres.)

F. *(Pronouncing it wrong.)* Canape?

B. *Bright green meadow. Everyone dressed in white.*

A. *(Dazed.)* I'm sorry?

F. *(Holding up a tray.)* Canape.

A. *(Correcting him, lightly.)* Oh, canapé.

F. *(Not realizing he's being corrected.)* Yeah. Make sure you get one with lots of roe.

A. Oh, I'm actually a little queasy?

F. *(Putting it together.)* You're the one getting married.

B. *It occurs to you this is true.*

A. Guilty.

F. Is it your first time?

A. Yeah, why do you ask?

F. Oh I just mean you're not—I mean you're not exactly…

A. A blushing bride?

F. Well

A. It's okay. I'm fifty-five.

F. *(His mind is blown.)* Wow.

A. Yeah. It kind of hits you like a truck.

F. I'll watch out. *(Beat.)* For the truck.
 I'm gonna— *(He moves to go.)*

A. Off you go.

(BARRY enters, played by ACTOR C.)

F. Canape?

C. No thanks.

> *(The* **CATER WAITER** *exits. The following a kind of game. Deadpan-flirty:)*

C. Say. Aren't you the one getting hitched?

A. That's right.

C. Who's the lucky guy?

A. Some shmo from the Bible Belt. Trying to pass as a New Yorker.

C. Bible gays—better watch out.

A. It's okay, I'm into guilt. His mother though, she's a piece of work.

C. He's worth it, though?

A. Sometimes.

C. Well if it doesn't work out, you just give me a call.

A. Forward.

C. I knows what I likes.

A. What do you likes?

C. Neurotic, fifty-something writers with a little meat on their bones and a healthy aversion to the outdoors.

A. Keep talking.

C. Especially writers whose short stories were once overlooked by a mainstream literary culture that looks down its nose at *genre*, but are finally starting to attract a passionate following.

A. That is a very specific fetish.

C. Lucky you.

> *(**D** floats by, an unidentified wedding guest. She squeezes them.)*

D. You two look so handsome—Congratulations!

> *(And she's gone, as quickly as she came. They drop the game:)*

A. Hi husband.

C. Hi husband.

(They take each other by the hand.)

You nervous?

A. Not yet.

> (**ACTOR C** *sees* **ACTOR E** *rushing in as the harried* **WEDDING PLANNER***:)*

C. Brace yourself.

E. We're out of champagne. I'm not gonna say your friends are lushes, but—

A. They are, they're lushes.

E. Open the Prosecco?

A. Yeah.

> *(The* **WEDDING PLANNER** *is already heading out – maybe he never broke his stride. Shouting to an unseen underling:)*

E. Do it!

> (**A** *and* **C** *survey the guests.)*

A. *(Nervous.)* People aren't eating, why aren't they eating.

C. They're eating.

A. Maybe the mini *bánh mì* were too exotic.

C. I don't know, I don't care, it's our wedding.
There's my mom. We should probably—

A. Hide?

C. *("You're terrible.")* See how she's *doing*.
She's a harmless old lady who wants you to feel comfortable with her.

A. Comfort. From the woman who wears a sequined gold sheath to a daytime wedding—

C. I know, it's a lot—

A. She's like an Emmy Award with a Tampa accent.

C. Well, you're not marrying *her.*

A. I sort of am.

C. *(Taking him by the arm.)* C'mon.

A. Barry wait—can we just stay here a moment? Just 'til the world stops spinning?

C. We could be waiting a long time.

B. *You take a mental snapshot of Barry. What's left on top of his head is grey, and his eyes disappear when he smiles.*

A. I'm just trying to—hold on to this.

C. That's why we hired a photographer.

A. I'm serious. The present is so—fast.

*(The **CATER WAITER** is here again.)*

F. Short-rib lollipops?

A & C. No thanks.

*(The **WAITER** exits.)*

A. He looks just like one of my exes.

C. Yeah?

A. It's kind of unnerving.

*(The **WEDDING PLANNER** rushes back in:)*

E. Okay people, we're five minutes away.

A. Wow. Wow.

C. *(To **E**.)* His head just exploded.

E. *(To **A**.)* You'll be fine.

A. *(To **C**.)* I'm gonna just—pee preemptively. *(To **E**:)* His mom's reading like half of Corinthians.

> *(Classical music starts to play—not "Pachelbel's Canon," but something that says the ceremony is imminent.)*

C. Hurry.

A. I am!

C. Don't try to escape out the bathroom window.

A. Ha ha.

B. *On the way to the bathroom, you pass everyone you ever met.*

A. Hi. Hi. Hey there.

F. *Your palms are sweating. Hand on the bathroom door.*

E. *As soon as the doorknob's in your hand, you know you've held it before*

D. *But you can't think where—*

> *(Lights shift. Continuous into:)*

IX.

C. *On the other side of the door is darkness. Darker than any room you've ever been in.*

D. *Somewhere far away, a radio plays a mariachi song.*

A. Hello?

> *(He listens a moment as the song plays.)*

Hello out there?

C. *There was something in your hand. Something many-edged and cool. Something you were supposed to remember...*

X.

E. Come in.

D. *Same bright office. Same big desk.*

E. Sorry to keep you waiting. I'm between secretaries— obviously.

D. *A row of girls just like her lined up outside.*

B. Oh god, don't even think about it—I'm just so pleased for this opportunity to meet you.

E. Well you didn't brave rush hour on the 405 just to *meet* me. If you want the job, you should say it.

B. I want the job.

E. You can't be coy in this town, Miss Griggs.

B. That's sage advice, Mr. See.

E. You can call me Mr. See.

D. *A moment of confusion.*

B. Okay.

E. Are those Louboutins?

B. You like?

E. *("Yes.")* That's test number one—a well-turned out foot. Pity 'bout your nails though.

B. I'm not really a pedicure kind of girl.

E. You work for me, you're a pedicure kinda girl.

B. Yes sir.

D. *The girl's eyes pass over a bald spot on his desk. Little circle of unfaded wood, as though it housed an object gone missing.*

B. Maybe you should tell me what you'd expect of me as your assistant.

E. I'll decide what to tell you.

B. Yes, Mr. See.

D. *He looks at her résumé.*

> *(Actually he keeps his eyes fixed on her—there is no résumé.)*

E. Phi Beta Kappa.

B. I worked hard.

E. Overseas program. Istanbul?

B. My minor was Byzantine art. You know, offset the whole cynical Communications pre-MBA—

E. Smart. Do any drugs?

B. I'm sorry?

E. Do you do any drugs, Miss Griggs.

B. You mean like medication?

E. You know what I mean.

B. No sir, I'm clean.

E. *(Disappointed.)* I see.

B. *(Trying to recover.)* I tried mushrooms once. Tasted terrible. I spent most of the afternoon hugging a tree. So on the nose, right? *(Getting a bit lost in it again:)* The moss was like a whole world.

E. You might wanna think about acquiring some uppers. That's pretty much how things get done around here.

B. Long hours.

E. Yes ma'am. My last assistant, sometimes she spent the night here. Right over there on her yoga mat. Good for the back, Rosie would say.

B. I bet she was a real ace.

D. *This hangs in the air.*

B. A reeeal ace.

D. *Is she mocking him?*

E. *(To* **B.***)* She sure was, until last Friday she just up and never came back. Just *(He makes the "poof" gesture from the earlier scene.)*—into thin air.

B. My brother disappeared like that,

D. *she says, taking a little risk.*

B. We were playing hide and seek. *(Tragic:)* He won.

E. I'm sorry.

B. I haven't given up yet.

D. *The hint of a challenge in this.*

E. I see.

D. *Mr. See takes one more look at her unpedicured toes.*

E. Who are you, really?

B. Jane Griggs, like it says on the resume.

E. I don't think so, Miss Griggs. You know what I think? I think you're as fake as those Louboutins.

B. What do you mean, these / set me back—

E. Louboutins have red soles. Those, as you see, are taupe.

D. *Shit.*

E. Plus, your Vuitton bag only has one "t."

D. *Shit.*

E. Clear Chinatown knock-off.

(Beat. Then, coming clean:)

B. Sixteen years, Mr. See, and not a trace of my brother.

D. *She kicks the fake Louboutins across the room and puts her feet on his desk, like a lazy cop.*

B. Sixteen years. Then out of the blue, on my Google Alerts: "Firelight Pictures Reaches First-Look Deal With Kai Shearwater." So you see, I just *had* to meet the man in charge.

E. Rosie didn't really burn out, did she. You've done something to her.

B. All I did was put some more Adderall in her Adderall.

E. Jesus.

B. I just gave her more of what she wanted. She's tied up in her closet, babbling about the Miss Arkansas pageant.

E. Impressive. Maybe I *should* hire you.

B. I'm just here to find my brother, Mr. See—or take you down trying.

E. He must've been a good brother.

B. He wasn't good or bad—he was just my brother.

E. Could it be you've made him perfect in hindsight? The way we do with dead people?

B. You don't know he's dead.

E. *(Crafty.)* Do you even remember him? Or do you just think you do?

D. *Anna Bell steels herself for the counterattack.*

E. Is it even him you miss? Or do you miss the way things were when he was alive? The way you were.

D. *Anna Bell rips one of the legs off his desk.*

E. Jesus!

> *(A low, frictive sound underneath the following, like metal on metal:)*

D. *She takes the leg and scratches one long, terrible wound around the wall of the room, like someone keying a car.*

E. What the hell are you doing?

B. You don't ask the questions anymore you piece of shit.

> *(Thunder. Continuous into:)*

XI.

*(The **FISHERMAN** atop his lamppost.)*

C. *Cabin Boy!,*

A. the First Mate shouts from the wheel. The whole sky red
   now.

C. *Josef!*

(Another clap of thunder.)

A. Before you can take a single step, a great wave knocks
   two good men overboard.

C. *Lash yourself to the staysail or you're next to Davy Jones!*

F. *Which one is the staysail?* you shout, drinking a gallon of
   salt water.

C. *Port side of the skysail!*

F. *Which one's the skysail!*

C. *Just shy of the moonraker!*

F. By now you've drunk another five gallons, but you bolt
   for the nearest staysail, the ground alive under you;
   the ground drunker than the First Mate that night
   he called you Nancy by mistake, "Pretty Nancy from
   Norwich" you remember as you lash the rigging round
   your ankle. Faster than you can finish the thought,
   the staysail snaps free of the mizzen and you're taken
   like a leaf in the wind, shooting high over the ship,
   stomach in throat. It would be almost fun if your life
   weren't about to be over. Then *splash,* you're down in
   the drink, under the ship, a keel-hauling performed
   by nature; lucky you know enough to swim down
   deeper so the barnacles don't cut you to ribbons. And
   just like that you're airborne again, the water flying
   off your hide like a wet dog getting dry; hand at your
   boot, on instinct, where it finds your favorite dagger
   for cutting you free. Headfirst falling now you jack out
   your right arm hoping anything will stop your fall and
   you end up with a handful of mermaid breast. Not a
   warm, welcoming mermaid breast but a hard wooden

mermaid breast that nearly snaps your wrist; your left hand finds her right breast and you're dangling from the prow by both breasts, a picture that would go down in seafaring lore if anyone lived to tell. And now the prow liberates itself from the stern—she's shaking you free, that wily mermaid!—and your last fumbling grab as you freefall frees the great round crystal in the mermaid's eye; you're falling together now, you and the crystal, and you don't let go when you hit the water, and you don't let go all night. The great ship lost beneath the black water along with the First Mate, your only friend, your only father, your something else. (You never even learned his name for calling it out.) And still you hold onto the crystal, which gives off a faint light of its own even in the new-moon night. And the sea creatures come and nibble at its edges—long-eyed viperfish and luminous jellies who think they've found a mate, but you fight them off; and the waves churn and the salt in your mouth but you don't let go.

XII.

(The faint mariachi music returns.)

C. *Still you're sitting in the dark. Those faraway notes raining down on you like Chinese water torture.*

B. *Creak of a floorboard.*

A. Hello? Why can't I see anything?

D. Don't be a smart-ass, Mr. Kai.

A. No, really—I can't see my hand in front of my face.

D. You've been blind for five years.

A. Who are you?

D. This isn't your best day, is it.
    (This is pronounced "Pow-la":) I'm Paula. I look after you.

A. We're not related?

D. God no.

A. I can tell. You have a bit of an accent.

D. I'm from El Salvador but my English is good. Some people can't even tell. They think I'm just formal.

A. No, I can tell.

D. Sure, Mr. Kai.

A. My last name is Shearwater.

D. Yes, but to me you're Mr. Kai. I like to be different.

A. Why can't I feel my legs?

D. You lost them.

A. Lost them where?

D. They cut them off.

A. They who?

D. Doctors.

A. Why'd they do that?

D. To save you.

　　　　(Beat.)

A. Do I have anything left?

D. *(Chuckling a little.)* Two arms, to write. Two ears.

A. I'm a writer?

D. Oh yes.

　　　　(A longer beat.)

A. Do you go through this with me every day?

D. *(Gentle.)* Most days you remember a little more. Things come back to you. Gutting a fish with your father, when you were a boy. Your grandfather's pipe. Your wedding day. I think the far-back things come easier. Or maybe that's just where you'd rather be.
    Hold still now—

A. Ouch!

D. This won't take long.

A. Ouch! What are you doing?

D. Just plucking your ears—you don't want hairy ears, do you? Not on your big day.

A. My big day?

D. You don't remember? You're getting an award today, for writing.

A. An award for not being dead yet.

D. Something like that.

A. I have a lot of those?

D. You put them on the shelves above the toilet. That way all / the guests can see

A. *(Overlapping.)* All the guests have to see. Yes, it's coming back to me.

D. We should get going—if you're up to it. There's a luncheon.

A. Oh no

D. Overcooked salmon and German wine. That's what you always say.

A. Do I have to give a speech?

D. You recorded it, on video. On one of your good days.

> *(Beat.)*

A. Do I have any kids?

D. No.

A. But I have a wife?

D. *(With a little laugh.)* I don't think Barry would've let you call him that.

A. Barry. Are you saying I'm a gay?

D. Oh Mr. Kai, sometimes you just slay me.

A. "Would've." Past Conditional. So Barry is…

D. Dead, yes. You had thirty-three wonderful years together and now he's dead.

A. What got him?

D. He was just old.

A. Like me.

D. Like you.

A. How old am I?

D. Eighty-eight.

A. Eighty-eight. That's older than Grandpa was when he
    told me—When he told me—. What did he tell me?
    Why can't I remember?

D. Mr. Kai, you're crying.

A. What did you say your name was?

D. Paula. Like "Pow."

C. *You can't see how she punches the air with her fist to illustrate
    "pow."*

F. *She's done it so many times since moving here that she doesn't
    realize it's lost on a blind man.*

D. You try.

A. *Pow*-la.

D. Good.
    Now let's get you into your tux.

XIII.

C. *Mr. See keys in a secret code and the heavy door swings open.*

E. Satisfied?

D. *Anna Bell removes the table leg from between his ribs.*

B. Very.

D. *And she steps into the room.*

B. It has to be zero degrees in here…

E. On account of the active molecules. The cold air keeps
    them tame. I think of flies, the way they hibernate in
    the cold.

B. *(Contrary.)* I don't think of flies.

D. *As they walk, Anna Bell takes in the shelves, high above their
    heads.*

B. *(Awed.)* You can't see where they end even.

E. You're a lucky girl, Anna Bell. No civilian has ever laid
    eyes on this before. Some real Area 51 shit.

B. Look but don't touch.

E. You can touch whatever you like. I just can't guarantee your safety.

B. Is it ever just a straight answer with you?

E. It is and it isn't.

D. *Anna Bell gives the wall a frustrated kick. A Chinese mask rolls forward, toppling an ancient Egyptian top.*

E. Careful!

B. Sorry.

E. I am a custodian of magic forces, Anna Bell. Totems and talismans especially. You look at me and all you see is a bad-ass executive with the world between his teeth, but in a realer sense I am a humble custodian of magic. The threads that surround your life—that surround all lives?—they can get awfully twisted when you start playing cat's cradle. It takes a lean, hard, bottom-line-minded mind to maintain order. It takes a quick fuse. It takes a sharp bullshit detector. It takes an interest in supply and demand—In the market and what it can bear.

B. I thought magic was supposed to be—

E. Fun?

B. Well, magical.

E. Not when it's your job. *(Beat.)* I'm a busy man, Anna Bell. You have one minute. Within this hall, there is a duplicate of every magical device anyone ever used.

B. There's two of each?

E. We keep the doubles for tracking. Whichever object you pick will lead you to its twin. Pick correctly, and it may even lead you to your brother.

B. You mean I have to guess?

D. *Running her hand along a shelf, Anna Bell touches a scepter topped with an onyx, a horn of plenty, a purple crayon that ever so slightly glows, and a robe made entirely of snakeskin.*

E. We think of magic things as mute, like animals. But like animals, they talk to each other. They say, *How long have you been waiting for a new adventure? Will you cause trouble*

this time? Will you be helpful? And the answer is always
I don't know, I don't know…

B. What happens if I pick wrong?

E. Don't think too much. That's good advice for most
situations.

C. *Anna Bell closes her eyes and some of the fear goes away.*
Her hand touches something metal, then something like fur –

B. Ew!

C. *—then something light as cotton candy, and finally something*
many-faceted. Cool but not cold, familiar but not intimate.
Something she might have had in her hand before without
even thinking about it, fetching the table linens for her
grandmother—

B. This one. I want this one.

E. Are you sure?

B. Of course not.

C. *Her hand closes on the crystal.*

XIV.

A. *The crystal is still tight in your fist when you wake, half-dead,*
on a bed of brown kelp.

> *(**ACTOR F** looks into the darkness.)*

F. Sir! Are you out there?

A. *A chorus of birds answers.*

F. Sir!

A. *You walk 'til you no longer see the ocean. You build a house*
there. You build the crystal into the house.

C. *Still you can hear the ocean.*

> *(**ACTORS D** and **C** appear as young*
> **GRANDMOTHER** and **GRANDFATHER.**)*

A. *Fifty years go by and you sell the house to a young man and his*
wife, who will one day be grandparents.

F. I was once a Cabin Boy on a ship,

A. *you tell them.*

C. On a pirate ship?

F. On a pirate ship.

A. *…in the hopes that in telling the story you will be free of it. But instead you pull other lives in with you, down in the drink.*

F. Mind the doorknob,

A. *you say, on your way out.*

> (**ACTORS C** *and* **D** *look at each other, puzzled, as their light goes out.*)

You walk until time slows down. You find a lamppost to stand under. You pick the lamppost because it's less like the ocean, man-made.

F. *(A small defeat in this:)* Like the mast of a ship.

C. *Still you can hear the ocean.*

> (*It starts to rain lightly.* **JOSEF** *looks into the darkness towards* **KAI**, *just as he did in Scene 2.*)

F. Hello?

A. *You wait for your story to end, but it isn't ready.*

F. Hello out there?

XV.

D. Rosie lies bound and gagged on the floor of her walk-in closet, feeling quite forgotten. She has tried and she has failed to wriggle out of Anna Bell's cruel girl-scout knots. She takes an emotional inventory of her closet to keep herself entertained:

> (**ACTOR B** *appears in a pool of light as* **LANE HEATHERETTE**. *She holds up each item as it is described, with cool detachment.*)

Putty-colored Manolo Blahniks, worn the night she heard that Lane Heatherette got the Yarbrough Mentorship…

Raspberry beach cover-up, worn to the Brentwood pool party where Lane Heatherette made the biggest splash...

And who could forget the Swarovski-encrusted Vera Wang column she wore that storied night she lost the Junior Miss Arkansas Executive crown by the smallest margin ever to the likes of—wait for it –

B. *Lane Heatherette.*

> (**LANE HEATHERETTE** *smiles slightly, enigmatically, as her light goes out.*)

D. While she *seems* immobile, something is afoot in Rosie on a microbiological level: Her pupils un-dilate; her eyelids un-twitch; that dry patch of skin on her elbow goes unscratched by nervous fingers. And as the Adderall and Acid Reflux Roast drain from her system for the first time in years, Rosie starts to lose her razor's edge, her killer's instinct—and somewhere, another Rosie who is half an inch taller and two percent twinklier silently surpasses her, taking her place as a strong second behind Lane Heatherette.

And a strange thing—Rosie doesn't care. She has been supplanted, yes, and yet the world still spins and the demon lights of Los Angeles still burn and little girls in Little Rock still practice with their ventriloquist dummies. And right about now, Rosie, still gagged and bound in a closet in a condo on a side street in Silver Lake, floats out of herself and advances one rung on the spiritual ladder they learned about in fifth grade Social Studies—Gandhi and Jesus on the top rung, Ted Bundy in the basement. The past rushes in and Rosie is back at her desk at the front of Miss McGinn's fifth grade classroom:

> (**MISS MCGINN** *comes out of the darkness, holding a single sheet of paper. She is patient and dowdy and faintly angelic in a real way—even in this drag manifestation.*)

F. Class,

I am your teacher, Miss McGinn
Or was it Miss McGann.
Why am I holding a blank sheet of paper?
you might be asking yourselves.
Pretend that this is a picture of your soul.

Everyone begins their life with a smooth new piece of paper. Some of you, if you're very lucky, might still look like this on the inside. But you see, every time someone says something a little unpleasant to you, a little discourteous, this is what they're doing to your sheet of paper.

    (She crumples the page.)

And you try your best to smooth it back, to make it good as new, but you'll never be entirely smooth again.

    (She carefully smoothes the page.)

D. At the time, Rosie thought this was any old Do-Unto-Others lesson. It didn't occur to her that her teacher Miss McGinn or Miss McGann had already had her own piece of paper crumpled countless times. She wasn't just giving them a lesson on how to treat people—she was giving them permission to get hurt.

    (MISS MCGINN *shows us the page and its faint creases.)*

F. Every day, someone crumples your sheet of paper, and every night you try to get it smooth again. We'll never be done, but that's the balance we strike between innocence and experience. That's the effort that will make us human. *(Beat.)* Any questions?

D. And her wrists remain bound and the gag in her mouth, but Rosie is free.

XVI.

*(**B** and **C** speak in the direction of* **A.** *)*

B. *Still can't feel your legs. Still can't see a damn thing.*

C. *Rustles and whispers, a roomful of bodies.*

B. *Silverware.*

     (We hear microphone feedback.)

E. Ouch—sorry folks. I just wanted to say how most of us in the room have been touched in some way by Kai Shearwater—even if it was just him telling us our writing was crap. Some of us he even had to tell twice.

F. *Polite laughter.*

E. This was a man with no patience for precious little observations of everyday life.

C. *"Was." Even as you sit here they're past-tensing you.*

E. Here was a man who believed in righteous fabulism—who believed you better fabulize or get the hell out of Dodge. After his one bitter taste of the Hollywood hack factory, he ran screaming back to his subconscious and that's pretty much where he stayed. His peers marveled at his childlike access to invention—like a kid making up whole worlds in his backyard. The purpose of writing, he once said, is to

    make

    shit

    up.

F. *Polite laughter.*

E. And nobody made up more shit than Kai Shearwater.

    Well, Mr. Shearwater. This award is for making the world a little more like the inside of your head.

D. They're standing, Mr. Kai.

A. Isn't that nice.

D. Everyone is standing for you.

A. At least that idiot isn't talking anymore.

D. I know.

A. Somebody should tell him the Beats are dead.

D. I know.

A. "Access to invention," what does that even mean?

All I did was rip off my grandpa's tall tales.

D. Here's your award, Mr. Kai. Careful, it's heavy.

A. Is this glass? Cheap bastards.

D. I think it's crystal.

A. You sure I haven't won this before? Feels familiar.

D. I think you can only get it once.

A. Ah yes, the Not-Dead award.

B. Excuse me, ma'am?

D. Yes?

B. This is going to sound kind of crazy, but I really have to talk to Kai?

D. If you want me to have him sign something for you, / I can—

B. No, I have to talk.

D. And you are…?

B. I'm his sister.

D. You're just a girl.

B. I told you it'd sound crazy.

D. *(Dismissing her.)* Thank you for paying your respects. I'll tell him you said hello.

B. Hey, what's that big bird over there?

D. What big bird?

B. Kai, it's Anna Bell!

A. *(Disoriented.)* Anna Bell?

B. I was hiding in the toy chest and you never found me. Remember? You were counting but you only got to ten.

A. I had a sister named Anna Bell. She was almost my age.

B. This might sound a little crazy, but I came here through a door in the office of a Mephistofilian studio executive using an exact duplicate of the doorknob that stole you out of our grandparents' sitting room seventy-eight years ago, the very doorknob that's sitting there in front of you, disguised as a lifetime achievement award. That's how it works—it stays with you every time you pass through a door. It's there to remind you, but that's not always enough.

A. You seem like a sweet girl, and I'm sure you're somebody's sister. But what you just described is the plot of my short story, "The Crystal Doorknob."

F. *What the*

C. *What?*

A. It's an early work. To be honest, it sounds a little plotty to me now.

B. That doesn't mean it's not true.

A. Sometimes people take my stories too seriously. Unfortunately they tend to be my best readers—the ones who lack boundaries.

B. Please, we were playing hide and seek—

D. I think you should stop bothering Mr. Kai. / This is a big day for him—

B. Just let me show him how the doorknob works.

A. I'm very old, I'm not looking for adventures.

B. This is the opposite of an adventure. This is going home. *(Beat.)* What if it could take us all the way back? Back to Grandpa and his stories, and Grandma's endless scarf, and Find My Booger?

A. *(Faintly familiar.)* "Find My Booger…"

B. And Gin Rummy! I'll let you win this time. I'll always let you win.

D. Please, don't confuse him. He has trouble with reality as it is.

B. *(To A.)* Please—

F. *Anna Bell takes your used-up old hands and places them on her face.*

A. What are you doing?

C. *This is not a surefire plan:*

F. *Coming to blindness late in life, and being a natural cynic, your stomach always turns at this particular brand of blind-person scene.*

C. *But your fingers find her strong, stubborn chin; the wide, Nordic planes of her cheeks, now trimmed of their baby fat; and the eyes a little too closely set, the first lines of permanent concern between them.*

A. Anna Bell. It *is* you.

B. Told you, stupid. Let's get you out of here.

D. Mr. Kai, where are you going?

A. Thank you for everything, Paula!

C. *Your chair already speeding, the crystal in your lap, your long-lost sister breathing down the back of your neck as she breaks into a sprint.*

F. *You can hear the women jumping to their feet, sequins flying; the men in tuxedoes falling away like dominoes.*

D. Help! She's kidnapping Mr. Kai!

E. Stop her!

B. Door, door, there must be a... *There!*

F. *The chair makes a hairpin turn.*

B. I've gotta send you through first. I'll be right behind you.

A. What if I lose you again?

B. Then I'll find you again.

E. Stop!

B. There's no time. Go! Go—

XVII.

A. On the other side of the door is nothing. Not darkness, but nothing. Far as the eye can see. Where there was Kai there is nothing but nothing. Nothing isn't all bad, of course. Your joints don't ache anymore, and you don't have to think about the effort of your next breath. You are beyond fear. Beyond the sea creatures who inhabit the edges of old maps.

XVIII*.

D. *Crisp autumn day in Green-Wood cemetery. A young Minister, who didn't know the deceased, addresses a small crowd.*

C. Thank you, Mrs. Juarez, for that lovely remembrance. And now we will hear a few words from Mr. Shearwater's own sister, Anna Bell.

>*(**ANNA BELL** comes into the light—she is an old woman with a walker now.)*

E. *The crowd makes way for a very old lady.*

B. Sorry, this is as fast as I go these days.

E. *Her eyes cataracted, but still somehow bright.*

B. Sorry. This is Mach 10 for me.

>*(She's at the front now.)*

Well. I was never the speechmaker in the family, my brother was. But I thought it might be nice to read a passage from his story "The Crystal Doorknob." The bit near the end, after the girl pushes her brother through the last door.

>*(The **MINISTER** takes out a paperback and sets it before her. On the cover: "Firelight Tales, by Kai Shearwater.")*

B. Thank you, dear. *(To the crowd again:)* This was one of Kai's first stories to get any attention. I think it embarrassed him a little when he got older—too much *plot*, he said. And he wasn't maybe as fancy as the author in the story, he wasn't collecting lifetime achievement awards. But it's always been one of my favorites—maybe 'cause he put me in it. And anyway too bad, big brother, you can't stop me now.

>*(To herself:)*

Is that the page? Yes.

---

* *Note: A new feeling of reality in this scene. Maybe we see a degree of visual detail we didn't see before. (In the Humana production, for example, autumn leaves were scattered on the stage.)*

(She starts to read.)

B. *"On the other side of the door, you feel a weight has been lifted…"*

> *(As she reads, the crystal doorknob, lying on the ground somewhere, starts to glow.*** *In its light, we can just make out* **JOSEF THE FISHERMAN**, *standing under his lamppost, and* **KAI**, *a boy again, standing a way's off. The way we first saw them, way back in Scene 2.)*

B. *"Your joints don't ache anymore, and you stand taller, and you don't have to think about the effort of your next breath."*

A. Am I a boy again?

B. *you ask, out loud, to no one in particular. To your surprise, somebody answers:*

F. At long last, he speaks!

A. What do you mean, at long last? I just got here.

F. You've been standing there in the shadows long as I can remember.

A. *(Disoriented.)* I came through a door. I was in a chair. My sister was pushing me.

F. I haven't seen her.

A. She was right behind me.

F. How old are you?

A. Ten, I think. Or Twenty-seven. I've been a lot of different ages today.

F. I see.

A. Are you a sailor?

F. In another life I was.

A. *(Childlike.)* On a pirate ship?

F. On a pirate ship.

> *(Beat.)*

A. Are we dead?

** *Note: I suspect that this is the first time we've actually seen it.*

F. *(The best he can answer.)* I think...everything has already happened to us.

> (**KAI** *looks at the doorknob. Maybe he moves to pick it up.*)

My mermaid's eye.

A. Do you think, can it take me back home? Back to where I started?

F. Think of how many doors there are in the world.

A. *(Sad.)* I know.

F. Think of how much you know. No little boy can know that much.

> (**KAI** *looks down at his feet.*)

Hey now, don't look so sad. Let me tell you a secret— Something that helps me when I get to missing the way things were.

A. What is it?

F. Lean close, I have to whisper it.

> (*As* **JOSEF** *whispers into* **KAI***'s ear,* **ANNA BELL** *speaks for him—she doesn't need the book anymore:*)

B. *We can be innocent twice, the Fisherman whispers. The first innocence we are given; the second we have to fight for.*

A. Fight how?

> (**JOSEF** *starts to lean in again.*)

Can't you just say it out loud?

B. *From up close, the old fisherman smells of fish and his whiskers are wet.*

F. Some things are easier to hear if you whisper.

> (**JOSEF** *whispers in* **KAI***'s ear.*)

B. *We must smooth our page, the Fisherman tells you, every night and every day, until all the wrinkles are gone. Until it looks like the page of a ten-year-old boy a little bored on a distant summer afternoon, wishing his life would begin."*

> (**ANNA BELL** *closes the book. The light of the crystal goes out, and* **JOSEF** *and* **KAI** *are gone. She takes in the audience at the memorial service.*)

B. Smooth our page. I don't know what my brother meant by that, but I kind of like it.

> (*She smiles sadly.*)

Maybe when I'm older.

> (*Light fades.*)

End of Play